SECOND CHANCE

NIKI DUPRE BULLET MYSTERIES
BOOK 1

JIM RILEY

CHAPTER ONE

Becky Howard looked over her shoulder. The eight-year-old daughter of a United States Congressman didn't see the big man who was supposed to be guarding her. She fidgeted, unable to keep her hands still. The line at the concession stand at the Baton Rouge Zoo moved at a snail's pace. The girl wanted an ice cream cone in the worst way. The guard had strict orders to limit her diet to healthy foods. Becky's mother was a physical trainer before becoming the trophy wife of a politician. She insisted her only child eat the right foods in the proper amounts.

Becky sighed. Only one customer ahead of her. However, the lady must've been ordering for a football team. She kept adding items until it seemed like she had ordered the entire menu. Becky looked over her shoulder one more time. She giggled when she saw the bodyguard frantically running in the other direction, down by the elephant exhibit.

"Are you Becky Howard?"

She hadn't noticed the man approach.

"Who are you?"

"Sam," the man answered. "Your mother is in the parking lot and wants you to go with her to Chuck E Cheese for a pizza."

"Really?"

Pizza was at the top of the list of her favorite foods. However, it wasn't on her mother's diet plan for the small girl, and she wondered what would cause her mother to change her mind.

"We need to hurry," Sam said. "You know how busy your mother's schedule is these days."

"What about Mr. Carl?" Becky asked, referring to her body-guard. "I have to tell him where I'm going."

"I'll take care of that after you're in the car with your mother."

"What about my ice cream cone? Can I take it with me?"

"Of course," Sam replied. "You can eat it on the way."

Becky couldn't believe her good fortune. An ice cream cone and pizza on the same day! Unbelievable! She grinned as she walked out of the gate with Sam.

CHAPTER TWO

"How THE HELL could you let this happen?" Don Howard, the United States Congressman, turned beet red as he yelled at Carl. The bulging veins in his temples looked like they would explode.

"I don't know. Becky was there one minute, and then she wasn't. She's a resourceful girl."

"Don't try to blame my daughter. It was your responsibility to watch her. You'll never work in this state again. I'll make sure of that."

"C'mon, Mr. Howard. Becky probably found a friend. I bet they're eating cookies right now."

FBI agent Sheila Richardson burst into the room. Her agency became involved due to Don Howard's status in Congress. She was the Special Agent in Charge, known as the SAC, in Baton Rouge. With a case this big, she desired center stage.

"You've got to see this, Don."

She used the representative's first name to let him know she was on his side.

"What is it, Agent Richardson?"

"We've got your daughter on tape leaving the zoo."

"Was she alone?"

"She was with a guy. He avoided the old cameras, but we caught him on a new one. We only got the two of them from the back."

"Who is he?"

"No idea yet, sir. We didn't get a shot of his face, so our recognition software does us no good."

"Is he white, Black, Asian, Hispanic? Can you at least tell me what ethnic group the monster belongs to?"

"We haven't determined that, and we're still working on it."

"I want my daughter back."

"Sir, we're doing everything humanly possible. There are limits to what we can accomplish."

"That's not what your director said when he came begging for more money in front of my committee. They told us you guys work miracles every single day."

"We're proud of our accomplishments, Don. We just heard about your daughter an hour ago, and we've already found the footage of her leaving the zoo."

"I don't care about the footage, Agent. I want my daughter."

The phone rang, startling all three in the room. It was a call that would change the entire direction of the investigation.

CHAPTER THREE

"WHO IS THIS?"

The call came in on Don Howard's personal cell phone, displaying an unknown number. Only a few people close to the congressman knew his private number.

"Hello, Congressman. May I speak to Agent Sheila Richardson?"

"You're speaking to me and nobody else, asshole. What have you done with my daughter?"

"If you don't let me talk to Agent Richardson, you'll never see Becky again. That would be a shame because she's a good little girl."

Don's anger at the caller released a string of expletives. Sheila Richardson frantically tried to get her fellow agents to trace the call. They could track a call in seconds instead of minutes. She made a motion with her hands, rolling one over the other. She wanted Don to keep the man talking. She finally caught Howard's attention, and he nodded.

"How can I get Becky back?"

"You need to allow me to talk to Agent Richardson. Otherwise, little Becky will be an appetizer for my pet alligator."

The image of his only child being eaten by a huge reptile was more than Don Howard could take. His knees buckled, and he fell against the sofa in his living room. Sheila snatched the phone from his hand.

"This is Agent Richardson. To whom am I speaking?"

"Hello, Sheila. Are you still drinking too much?"

"What? How do you know that?"

"I know everything about you. You were a high flier until the Agency discovered your problem with the bottle. That's why they shipped you out to the boondocks."

"Baton Rouge isn't the boondocks."

She tried to extend the conversation any way she could.

"Then why did you beg them not to ship you here if it's such a wonderful place to live?"

"You seem to know a lot about me. Tell me more about yourself. I don't even know your name."

"How quickly we forget our friends, Sheila. And to think, I still have a picture of you in my bedroom. I look at it every night."

Sheila nervously looked around. This call wasn't being recorded, and no one thought Don's personal cell phone would be how the kidnapper would make contact. She was in a quandary. If the congressman found out his daughter's kidnapping resulted from a deranged man's anger toward the agent, her future looked bleaker than ever.

"Give me a hint. I still don't know who you are."

"Tell your guys to relax, Sheila. It'll do them no good to trace this call. It's a waste of time."

"Why did you take Becky?"

"Two reasons," the man replied. "The first is money. I like

money. You like money. That's why you invested in that Ponzi scheme. You're greedy."

Shocked by his statement, the agent felt her knees weaken. No one knew about her poor investment. She was too ashamed to report her involvement. How did this man know?

"You said there are two reasons. What's the second?"

"I want the world to know just how screwed up you really are, and I want you to suffer."

"Why?" Richardson asked.

"You'll find out after you suffered enough. This is only the beginning. You're not going to like me much by the time I get through with you."

"What have I done to deserve this?"

A dial tone was the only sound left on the line.

She looked at her fellow agents. "Well? Did you trace the call?"

The older agent stepped forward.

"Yes, ma'am. We know the point of origin of the call."

"So, why are you standing there? Get moving! Why don't we have units on the way?"

"We can't, ma'am. The call came from the bottom of the Mississippi River. Eighty feet below the surface."

CHAPTER FOUR

"WHO IS THIS GUY?" Howard asked.

"We're not certain at this point, Don."

"It sounds like he knows you."

Sheila had given the congressman and the agents a brief overview of the phone call. She left out the part about the Ponzi scheme. It was embarrassing enough for her to be part of the reason for the abduction.

"I don't know from where. I didn't recognize his voice."

"How much money does he want?"

"He didn't say. I've seen this before. The kidnapper is trying to knock us off balance."

"I must congratulate him because he's done a helluva job doing just that. What's next?"

"He'll call back. He has to tell us how much he wants and how to deliver it."

"He's way ahead of you, Agent Richardson. I'm not sure I feel comfortable with you being involved."

She flinched when he used you instead of the FBI as a

whole. He had pointed a finger directly at the Special Agent in Charge.

"We're the best you can get, sir. I don't see where you have many options."

"I can hire Niki Dupre," Don said flatly.

Sheila shuddered. She knew the reputation of the strawberry-blonde private investigator. Niki was an icon in South Louisiana. Whenever law enforcement failed, Niki Dupre was on speed dial. Inevitably, the PI found the truth when other efforts came up short.

"Sir, we have the best technology and people available. Miss Dupre has nothing to offer in this situation."

"How come the kidnapper knows more about you than you do about him? Can you answer that?"

Sheila didn't know what to say. She asked herself the same question with no answer available.

CHAPTER FIVE

"HI. I'M NIKI DUPRE."

Sheila looked at the long-legged woman with thick hair. She grimaced. No wonder every man in Baton Rouge would rather have the private investigator on the case instead of the plain-looking FBI agent. To rub salt in an open wound, Niki was reported to be as smart as she was attractive. Maybe more so.

"I'm Special Agent in Charge Sheila Richardson."

The homely agent extended her hand. She normally didn't think of herself as unattractive. However, in the presence of Niki Dupre, Sheila felt like an ugly older sister.

"Congressman Howard invited me to consult on the case. I hope I'm not intruding."

"As a matter of fact, you are. I can see no way you can make a positive contribution."

"Perhaps I should talk to Don," Niki said. "He was adamant about my involvement."

"You'll just get in the way. With a little girl's life at stake, I don't think you should be here."

"Tell me what you have so far. I'll let Don know if I can help him and Becky."

Sheila shrugged. She gave Niki a short description of the abduction and the phone call. She left out the information on the Ponzi scheme.

"Where does he know you from?"

"I don't know. He may be making up a story to throw us off."

"But, according to your version of events, the kidnapper asked for you without Don telling him you were involved. How would he know?"

Sheila shook her head.

"I don't know, and to be blunt, I don't care. It's not relevant to the case."

"How can it not be? He gave you two reasons for his actions, and one was you."

"I believe he's bluffing. I think he's trying to send us down the wrong rabbit trail."

"Why go to all that trouble if this is only about money? Can you explain that to me?" Niki asked.

"Because he wants us looking somewhere else while he takes the money and runs. If we're chasing a phantom connection with me, he'll get away clean."

Niki shook her head.

"I'm not buying it. Plus, you haven't told me the entire conversation. What else did he mention about your private life?"

"Huh? How could you possibly discern that from what I told you?"

"You're body language told me more than your words. You're concealing part of the conversation and afraid he'll make it public."

If Sheila was impressed before, the agent was now astounded. At Quantico, Richardson had been at the top of her class in reading body language. She could always tell when a classmate was telling a lie in the prescribed sessions. None ever knew if Sheila was lying or telling the truth when she was on the other side of the desk. Even the retired agent teaching the course admitted he couldn't discern any discrepancies in Richardson's stories.

But this private citizen had seen right through her. The agent had two choices. She could continue to withhold the secrets or give them up.

"I don't know what you're talking about," Sheila said firmly. "I've told you everything you need to know."

"No, you haven't," Niki insisted. "This is a guess, but I believe it has to do with your drinking problem."

Sheila's knees had felt weak while talking to the kidnapper. Now they were useless. She collapsed onto a loveseat and stared at Niki like she was looking at a ghost. The agent wanted to say something in denial. No matter how hard she tried, nothing came out. She stammered while Niki remained silent. Finally, Sheila dropped her head into her hands. Tears flowed down the agent's cheeks.

"I'm sorry," Niki said. "If I'm gonna be helpful, I have to know the truth. All of it."

"I had a problem," Sheila said. "I don't anymore."

Niki remained silent.

"Okay," Sheila said. "I still have a problem now and then."

"Now we're making progress," Niki said. "Tell me everything the kidnapper said."

CHAPTER SIX

AFTER SHEILA FINISHED with the narrative, Niki sat back, deep in thought. For several minutes, the two sat in silence.

"Do you know why this man wants to bring you down?"

"None." Sheila shook her head. "I've made a few mistakes, but nothing to deserve this."

"Think back through all your cases. There have to be a few that stood out in your mind."

"A few," Sheila said. "I might have used some evidence..."

The ring of her cell phone interrupted the sentence. The FBI agent frowned when she looked to see the caller ID.

"Hello?"

"Hey, Sheila. Are you and Miss Dupre having a good conversation about me?"

Shocked, Sheila paused before responding.

"How do you know she's here?"

"I know everything. I thought you would have realized that by now."

"If you want me, come after me," Sheila said. "Don't hurt an innocent child because of your feelings toward me."

"That would be way too easy. What would the agency think after you blow this and get little Becky killed?"

"Please don't hurt her. Take the money, and go to a foreign country. Just don't hurt Becky."

"It's not up to you, Sheila. However, for old times' sake, I'll make a deal with you."

"What kind of deal?"

"Tell Howard to put together five million dollars, and I want one hundred and twenty-three thousand from you."

"A hundred and twenty-three thousand?"

"That's how much you can take out of your savings plan, and it leaves you a couple hundred dollars."

"How do you know this?"

"How many times do I have to tell you, Sheila? I know everything about you."

"But how?"

"That doesn't matter. Tell Miss Dupre I'm going to call her."

CHAPTER SEVEN

SHEILA ENDED HER CALL, and Niki's cell rang. Niki pressed the button but said nothing.

"Cat got your tongue, Miss Dupre?"

Niki offered no reply.

"I see." The man sighed. "You're giving me the silent treatment. My ex-wives used to do that to me."

Niki maintained her silence.

"I just wanted to tell you that your contribution to the kitty will be one million dollars."

"No."

"Don't mess with me. Do you want to be responsible for Becky's death?"

"I won't be," Niki replied. "It's your decision alone to decide if Becky lives or dies."

"You're mistaken. Little Becky will live if you, Sheila, and the good congressman do everything you're supposed to do. If you don't..."

"I already know you plan to kill Becky no matter what anyone does."

"And how would you know that?"

"The same way I know you're from Baton Rouge, and you haven't had multiple wives."

The caller met Niki's pronouncement with silence.

"Cat got your tongue?"

"You know nothing about me. All you're doing is blowing smoke."

"Your denial means I'm right. Before much longer, I'll know if you wear boxers or briefs."

A dial tone sounded on the other end of the line.

CHAPTER EIGHT

"How DID YOU DO THAT?" Sheila asked. "How can you know he's a local and has no ex-wives?"

"The first part is easy," Niki said. "He said *just* instead of *only*. That means he's probably from the south. Since Baton Rouge has been your only station down here, it makes sense that's where the kidnapper lives."

"I don't know. It seems like a stretch."

"Perhaps." Niki nodded. "But his reaction told me I was dead on the mark."

"And the ex-wives thing?"

"His tone changed when he said his ex-wives, which means he lied about that part. My guess is he's still married to his first wife."

Sheila shook her head.

"Remind me to never play poker with you. I'd be afraid to bluff."

Don Howard walked into the office. Sheila looked at the congressman and then focused on the whiskey glass he held in his hand.

"I heard you both talking," he said. "How much does he want?"

"Five million from you," Sheila responded. "One hundred and twenty-three thousand from me."

Howard's face contorted into a look of questioning.

"That's how much I can withdraw from my savings plan," Sheila explained. "I don't know how he knows that."

Don looked at Niki.

"And he wants money from you?"

"He asked for a million. I refused."

"Don't. I'll pay you both back. Call him back and tell him you've reconsidered."

"Don," Niki said softly. "I believe this guy is already determined to kill Becky no matter what we do. You'll waste your money if you pay him."

"I can't take that chance, Niki. I couldn't sleep at night knowing I treasured my money more than my daughter."

Niki nodded. She also realized he would blame her if he and Sheila paid and Becky died. The money meant nothing to the long-legged investigator. She had millions in the bank. Niki's resistance was based on her reading of the kidnapper. He had a plan, and it was going without a hitch. That is, until Niki refused to pay. Therefore, she wasn't surprised when Don Howard's phone rang.

"Hello."

Don listened to the caller for several minutes without saying a word.

When he hung up, he turned and said, "I'm sorry, Niki. You're fired."

"Firing me won't change his mind, Don. If that makes you feel better, I'll pay the million, but it won't change the outcome."

"Please don't make this more difficult than it already is. Please leave my house."

"Call me when this is over," Niki said. "I'll help you find Becky's murderer."

CHAPTER NINE

SHEILA LOOKED AT DON.

"He said something to you, didn't he?"

"He told me to gather the money. He'll call at six tomorrow with instructions for delivery."

"I don't know if I can get my money that quickly," Sheila said. "I don't have that much lying around."

"I can put it together. He knows your dilemma, and he said for you to make the submission for withdrawal, which will give him enough proof."

"How will he know if I do or don't? It's not like transactions in my savings plan are public."

"How does he know all this? It's almost like he has a camera following us around," the congressman replied.

"That wouldn't account for him knowing about my past. Unless he's been recording me for years."

"Perhaps he has. Maybe his animus toward you started when you were still in Virginia."

"But Niki said he's from Baton Rouge."

"Do you believe her?"

"I don't know. She sure sounded convincing, and I'd hate to be in a position to bet against her."

"Well, I don't believe her," Don said. "She's nothing but a private investigator, and I'm not sure why I called her in the first place."

"Because you love Becky," Sheila responded.

"I know, but I should have trusted you and the agency. She's nothing but local help but we don't have to worry about her anymore."

"The FBI has your back, Don. We'll make sure no one will hurt Becky."

CHAPTER TEN

Don left Sheila alone while he made arrangements to collect the considerable sum of money. Despite her confident statements, she felt anything but. The kidnapper, whoever he was, knew way too much. Her past. Her present. The company she was with.

Sheila was processing this information when inspiration came to her.

She called to the other agents.

"Guys. Come in here."

Two agents immediately responded and appeared in the doorway, their previous responsibilities no longer a priority.

"I want you to sweep this room. I want to know if anyone is bugging it with audio or video."

She observed as they went about their job. Both men had years of experience and knew their jobs better than Sheila. It was best for her to stay out of their way. They used a wand to scan every nook and cranny, piece of furniture, and light fixture. They searched the entire room, and despite all their efforts, found nothing.

"Nothing? I don't understand how else he would know I was talking to Niki Dupre."

"Maybe he's got a hyperbolic microphone."

"He'd have to be standing right outside the window," Sheila responded. "We would have seen him."

"We've got some that will reach out for over a mile with the right antenna under the right conditions."

"But that's us." Sheila shrugged. "We're talking about a regular citizen here."

"Not to question your judgment, ma'am, but are you sure?"

Sheila shuddered at the thought of what he implied.

"No. I guess I'm not."

CHAPTER ELEVEN

THE CALL to Sheila's cell came at 5:32 the next evening as the bags of money were being loaded into an SUV. The FBI parked it, along with a guard, inside Don Howard's garage.

"Hey, sweetheart," the man said. "I hope you had an extremely productive day."

"Get on with it."

Sheila's nerves had already frayed, and she had no patience for his tomfoolery.

"Tsk, tsk. Do you not enjoy having a discussion with an old friend? I hope you're not drinking again."

"It's none of your business what I do. Where do you want the money delivered?"

"And I thought we might be friends." The man laughed. "After all this is over, why don't you let me buy you a drink. We'll see what develops from there."

"I don't accept drinks from scumbags," Sheila said. "Tell me where you want the money taken."

"C'mon, sweetheart. Are you like this in bed? All business

and no foreplay? If you work with me, I can show you how to have a real good time."

"The only good time I'll have with you is to watch you marched off in shackles to Angola."

"Now we're getting somewhere. I didn't know you liked chains and cuffs. I've never tried them, but I'm willing."

"I'm not," Sheila snarled. "Especially with the likes of you. Do you want me to deliver the money or not?"

A long sigh came from the other end of the line.

"If you insist. Maybe I can find a way to make your trip more interesting."

"It'll be interesting enough," Sheila said. "Hurry up. I'm tired of talking to you."

"Whoa," the man said. "Let's not get confused as to who's giving the orders and who's taking them."

"I don't care. If you want the money, call me back."

Sheila disconnected the call. Barely a minute later, her cell rang again.

CHAPTER TWELVE

"Hello, scumbag. Are you ready to do business now?"

"Not until I teach you some manners first."

"How do you propose to do that?"

"Like this."

Sheila heard screams in the background. She had no doubt they came from Becky Howard.

"Please!" the child screamed. "Please don't!"

"Hold on," Sheila yelled into the cell.

Her pleas were answered by more screams of agony. She was sure she heard the snap of tiny bones through the phone. Becky let out one final sob before she went silent.

"You bastard! You didn't have to hurt her."

"I had to teach you a lesson," the voice said. "Besides, she doesn't need all ten fingers."

"If I find you, I'll see how you like it when I chop off..."

"You don't want me to snap off another, do you? If you keep this up, I'll remove all ten and then start on her toes. And it'll be your fault."

Sheila remained quiet but fuming. She wanted to vent her

anger at this madman. Though, that approach would only cause more torture for an innocent eight-year-old.

"I'll do what you want," Sheila said. "Where do you want me to bring the money?"

"Now that's better. See, I told you we could get along."

Sheila fought back the words she wanted to say. They would only bring harm to Becky.

"Go to the Walmart in Central. There's a bank of phones inside the door. Wait for one to ring."

The caller disconnected.

CHAPTER THIRTEEN

"What about Becky?" Don Howard asked. "How can we be sure he won't kill her?"

"Settle down," Sheila said. "The agency knows how to handle the situation. Nothing will happen to Becky."

She didn't mention Becky was missing one finger already.

"How will you handle it?"

"I'll have an agent in the car with me. Two more will follow in the tail car. We'll nail this scumbag."

"What if he spots the tail?"

"He won't. We're good at our job, Don. We won't let him do anything else to Becky."

"Else?" Don arched his eyebrows.

"In addition to the kidnapping."

"I thought you meant he had already hurt Becky in some way. Do you think he has?"

Sheila shrugged.

"I doubt it. He knows we'll track him down to the ends of the earth if he does."

"I wish I hadn't fired Niki. She would know what to do in this situation."

"She was in over her head, Don. You need to leave this to the professionals."

"What were you two talking about before I came in?"

"She made some wild guesses about the case. None were close to the truth."

"How will the tail car track you? The parking lot at the shopping center is always full of people."

"I've got a tracer on my car," Sheila said. "They'll know where I am, even if they can't see me."

"Did you put a tracer in with the money?"

"It's sewn into the strap of the duffle bag."

"How soon do you have to be at the phone bank?"

"I need to leave now."

"What if I get Niki to meet you there?" Don asked.

"Please. She's nothing, and she can do nothing. You need to forget about Niki Dupre."

CHAPTER FOURTEEN

"How are you doing so far?" Sheila asked with her hand over her mouth. She parked at the shopping center and didn't want anyone to see her talking to the agent in the back on the floor.

"I'm fine," the man whispered. "Can you leave the car running with the air on?"

"Sorry," Sheila whispered. "I'll try to hurry."

She got out of the SUV, looking at every car in the lot. She spotted a similar SUV in the far corner, a few hundred yards away. With a slight nod at the two tailing agents, Sheila went inside the sliding doors.

Eight public phones lined the wall. The kidnapper hadn't been specific about which one to stand by. She didn't have to wait long before the third phone rang.

"Hello."

"Did anyone follow you?" the caller asked.

"Of course not." Sheila tried to sound convincing. "I came alone, just like you instructed. I wouldn't take a chance of more harm coming to Becky for my mistakes."

"Very good. A small complication has arisen. I'll have to get back to you in a minute."

"Let's get this over with."

"Sorry. I have to take care of a little business first. By the way, that blue blouse looks good on you."

The man disconnected. Sheila stood with the phone in her hand for a long time. She stared out into the parking lot. The kidnapper could see her. How else could he know she wore a blue blouse?

The senior agent slammed the phone back onto the receiver. She spoke to the two agents listening through the hidden microphone under her lapel.

"Did you guys get that?"

"Loud and clear," came the response. "We're scanning the lot for a single man who looks suspicious."

"Make sure it's him. I don't want to spook him, and I don't want him to hurt Becky."

"We know how to do our job," the agent replied from the back of Sheila's car. "We'll find him if he's really here."

"He's here. I can feel it in my bones."

Sheila sat on the bench just inside the door. She didn't know what else to do. The kidnapper was the puppeteer, and Sheila was the puppet. With him watching, she felt trapped. Whatever she did, he pulled the strings.

An urge came over her to pull her weapon and charge into the parking lot. If she saw a single man looking in her direction, she wanted to empty the clip into him. The agent had gone through the scenario in her mind for the sixth or seventh time when the phone rang again.

"Hello."

"Sorry about the delay," the man said. "Now we're ready to go to step two of our merry little plan."

"I don't see the merriment."

"You need to get out more often. Why don't you let me buy you a drink tonight? I can afford it."

"You need to take the money and get out of town. You've already hurt Becky. The only time we'll share a drink is at the visitors' center in Angola."

"And I thought we were making progress in our relationship, Sheila. Now I'll have to reevaluate it."

"The only relationship I want with you is to give you the money, and you give me the girl."

"We're gonna do that," the man said. "I thought we could get beyond business. But you'll have to wear heels. Those flats aren't doing you any favors."

"Can we stick to business, please?"

"If you want to be a stick in the mud," came the reply. "If you look out, there's an Impala parked three spots down from your ugly SUV. Can you see it?"

Sheila had to lean back and stretch the metal cord as long as it would go. Finally, she spotted the Impala.

"The white one?"

"That's it, sweetheart. You don't mind if I call you sweetheart, do you? That's how I consider you, Sheila."

"What about the Impala?"

"All work and no play makes Sheila a dull girl."

"I don't care. What about the Impala?"

"That's your new ride," the kidnapper said. "Take the money out of your vehicle, and transfer it to the back seat of the Impala. Can you handle that?"

"There are three bags. I had to do that so I could pick them up. They still weigh fifty pounds each."

"Forty-four and one quarter each without the additional money from you. That'll add less than a pound to each bag."

"If you say so," Sheila said. "I'll put the money in the Impala. How do we get Becky?"

"Slow down a bit. This is called foreplay. You should try it if a man is ever attracted to you again."

"How do we get Becky? I'm not turning five million dollars over to you until I'm certain Becky is safe."

"Be patient, sweetheart. We're just starting step two. I want you to get into the Impala and drive away. Go to the Winn-Dixie on the corner of Hooper and Joor. The phones are outside the store."

The phone went dead.

"Did you guys get that?"

A muffled reply of *Roger* came back.

Sheila made a mental note to tell the agent not to talk with his hand over his mouth. In the far corner of the lot, no one would notice his lips moving. She called the agent in the SUV she had driven to the lot.

"Did you get that?"

"Yes, ma'am. What do you want me to do?"

"Nothing," Sheila replied. "This guy is obviously watching us."

"Roger, ma'am. Good luck."

"The other guys are watching my back. Call the office and get someone to pick you up."

CHAPTER FIFTEEN

SHEILA PACED BACK and forth outside the Winn-Dixie for over fifteen minutes, waiting for a phone to ring. It hadn't. To make matters worse, her microphone and receiver weren't working. She had no contact with the two agents in the tail car, and thought something might be wrong. She couldn't get the hidden agent in the SUV to respond, either. Since no agents could hear her or talk to her, she assumed the problem was with her equipment.

She couldn't see the two agents, but that meant little. They could be at the fast food restaurant across Hooper Road, or in the parking lot of the Baptist Church across Joor. They could keep an eye on her from either place with almost no chance of being spotted.

The sound of the phone startled her. She snatched it from the receiver.

"I'm here," she shouted.

"Good," the man said. "All that pacing will work off those love handles. Don't get too skinny, though. I like a little meat on my girls."

She couldn't help herself. Her heart began to pound as she turned and scanned the cars in the parking lot. He had to be there somewhere. He was watching every move. She heard the man laughing at her from the other end of the call.

"What's so funny?"

"You, sweetheart. I find you hilarious."

"Where is Becky? I'm tired of playing games."

"We'll get to that, darling. You need to calm down. If you have a heart attack, you won't help her."

"Just bring her to me and take the money. That's all I care about right now."

"I like it when your chest goes up and down like that. Very impressive."

"You..." Sheila tightened her lips, trying to keep the words inside. She was ready to tell him exactly what she thought.

"Go ahead, sweetheart. Tell me how much you love me."

"Where is Becky?"

"She's resting comfortably. Now, let's see if you can transfer the money to me appropriately."

"I'll do it any way you want," Sheila said. "I have to be sure Becky is safe before you get it."

"Are you familiar with the maze?"

"What maze?"

"It's an unfinished subdivision north of the grocery store. They put the streets in before the development company went bankrupt, and it's since become overgrown."

"How do I get there?"

Sheila listened as the kidnapper gave her directions. He ended the conversation by telling her what to do once she arrived.

CHAPTER SIXTEEN

AN OPEN GATE led into the sixty-two-acre site. Briars and brambles grew high in the ditches on the sides of the roads. Trash littered the streets until nothing but a small path down the middle was the only way to navigate through. Sheila drove past the first street to her right and crossed a small bridge. A hundred feet further, she came to a tee. Per the instructions given by the kidnapper, she turned left. After crossing another bridge, she came to a cul-de-sac. She stopped and waited, staring impatiently at her cell phone. The wait couldn't have been over ten minutes, though time moved so slowly for Sheila. It felt like ten hours. Each second crawled in slow motion. Joy to the World sounded from her cell.

"I'm here," she said.

"I know. I've been watching since you arrived. I hope you're alone."

"I am," Sheila said, wondering how far away her backup detail might be. Since her microphone and earpiece had malfunctioned, she had no idea. The agent didn't dare call them. The kidnapper gave every indication he was close and claimed to be watching her.

"Good. Becky is ready at the other end of the street you're on. Drop the money here, and go get her."

"No. I have to know she's safe, and I have to see her before I leave the money with you."

"C'mon, sweetheart. Don't you trust me after all we've been through together? You're cutting my heart out."

"Why don't I just get Becky? You're close enough to see what I'm doing."

"Seeing you doesn't mean I'm close. Technology is amazing these days."

"How can I know Becky is safe?" Sheila asked.

"Hang up. I'll send you a live picture."

In less than a minute, the same song sounded again. When she opened the connection, a video streamed over the monitor. Sheila had never seen Becky Howard's face, but knew she was looking at the congressman's daughter. Becky's mouth was gagged with a white cloth, and she wore the same clothes she had on at the zoo. The only difference from the surveillance video at the zoo was a bandage covering the stub of the little girl's finger on her left hand. Sheila gasped at the sight of the bandage. Her stomach roiled at the thought of Becky's pain and for being the cause of her injury after verbally sparring with the kidnapper. Sheila vomited. The SAC could see her career fading before her eyes.

The third attempt to empty her stomach was the last for Agent Richardson. Sheila staggered back to the edge of the cul-de-sac. She looked back at her phone. Tears rolled down Becky's cheeks, and her eyes pleaded for help. The image from the video faded and left blackness covering both the phone and Sheila's soul. She felt as defeated as she had ever been in her entire life.

The agent jumped when the phone rang again. There was no joy in Sheila's world, despite the tune.

"Agent Richardson. I hope I've convinced you to take the terms of my offer."

"Yes. I'll leave two bags here. After I get Becky, I'll return with the third."

"Very good, sweetheart. I knew we were meant for each other, and now I believe that."

Sheila wanted to tell him exactly what she thought. If she could only spot the man. If he showed his face, she would empty her clip into his worthless body.

"Where do I go?" she asked.

"Drive back the way you came. Go to the end and stop where it makes it tee. Get out of your car, and walk down the lane to your left. It's not far. You'll see a gas pipeline."

"How do I find Becky?"

"Walk to your left on the pipeline. Becky won't be hard to spot."

Sheila took two bags of money and dropped them on the road. She left the third bag on the back seat. Emotionally spent, the agent drove back the way she had come. She passed the street she had used to enter the development. Sheila found two more streets on her right, though none turning to the left. After the fourth street, she saw the end of the road. She nervously continued driving and found another street to her right before finally finding a lane to her left. After scanning the area in all four directions, she tried contacting the agents in the tail car. Silence...

Sheila took a deep breath and exhaled slowly before stepping out of the Impala. She stared in all four directions, hoping for a glimpse of the kidnapper. No such luck. Sheila looked down at her hands. They shook so badly the agent couldn't have held a steady aim if the kidnapper had appeared. Sheila regained her composure and decided she never wanted to see him again when a thought struck her.

She took the third bag of money and dumped it into the trunk in case he tried to sneak up and steal the rest of the money from the backseat. She had to find Becky before more harm came to the innocent girl.

Her first steps down the short lane were unsteady. Sheila was never unsure of herself. No matter the circumstances, the agent always kept her cool. There was none left. Her brain and soul were on fire. Each step became more tortuous. Despite the video, Sheila didn't have a good feeling about Becky coming out of this alive. Niki Dupre had predicted the kidnapper would never let the girl live. The SAC formed a new respect for the long-legged investigator. She would have given anything to have Niki next to her. Sheila mentally kicked herself. Her desire to claim fame from the case might cause her downfall.

The lane was less than one hundred feet long but felt like a hundred miles to the agent. With every step, she expected to feel the impact of a sniper's bullet. Without the protection of her agents, she felt like a sitting duck. No shot came. Sheila reached the end of the lane where a six-inch pipe gate protected the gas pipeline. She climbed over and crossed a shallow ditch. She walked out into the open, making herself an easy target from any direction.

Sheila stood for over a minute, expecting her life to end at any second. However, there was only silence. A movement behind her made her jump. She turned with her pistol drawn, only to find an armadillo going about its business. The SAC smiled, looking at the mammal. A weird bit of trivia came to her mind. Armadillos were the only mammals other than humans able to contract leprosy. She laughed. Only a crazy person would think of that at a time like this.

The agent kept the pistol in her hand. If the kidnapper

attacked, she could fire back. The first step was the hardest. She expected a trap. How she wanted the agents for backup, and none were there. She was alone. She nervously took step after step, expecting to meet death with each one, all the while searching for some clue as to Becky's whereabouts. She saw something that didn't fit at the edge of the woods. The colors were wrong. It took a few minutes to recognize Becky's clothes from the trip to the zoo. Sheila sprang forward, forgetting her own danger. At five feet away, Sheila stopped and stared at the clothes. She knew why the clothes didn't look the same. They were covered with blood. Sheila stepped closer and discovered it wasn't just Becky's clothes on the ground but her body. A body without a head.

CHAPTER SEVENTEEN

SHEILA CALLED the office since she couldn't contact the two agents tailing her. In less than ten minutes, the area filled with law enforcement. Two teams of FBI agents arrived. Three squad cars from the East Baton Rouge Sheriff's Department joined them. A coroner's van parked next to the white Impala. A sedan arrived which Sheila didn't recognize. The driver was a huge man, almost a behemoth. The passenger, however, caught her attention. She recognized the man immediately. He was Ed Samuelson, the man forced to retire to make room for Sheila. As they walked up, neither guy looked friendly, which was to be expected from Ed. He wasn't ready to retire at only fifty-eight years old, but the agency needed a spot as far from Quantico as possible. That spot was Baton Rouge. The agency asked Ed to retire. When he refused, they retired him anyway.

The other guy looked like a replica of Goliath Sheila had seen in her Bible. He dwarfed the people around him, both in height and girth. He strode with a sense of authority.

"You guys can't be here," Sheila said.

"I'm Samson Mayeaux. I'm the chief of homicide for East

Baton Rouge Parish. I'll go anywhere I please in this parish.

"And I'm with Samson," Ed said from behind the massive cop. "He invited me to join him."

The situation was getting worse for Sheila. She couldn't resist the chief of homicide and the ex-SAC without ramifications. Having them breathing down her neck during the investigation was too much to bear... until a white Ford Explorer arrived at the scene.

If Sheila hadn't been sick when she found the body, she was about to be at the arrival of the strawberry blonde investigator. Niki Dupre walked up to Samson with a smile and hugged him. Or close to one. Even Niki's long arms couldn't extend around the chief's wide girth.

"Hey there," the attractive investigator said to Samson. "Why did you ask me here?"

"Because ol' Ed here thinks his agency is creating a cluster right under our noses," Samson replied.

Sheila gasped. The FBI was a closed society. None of its dirty laundry was ever aired. Now this monster talked openly about the agency's ineptitude.

"Sir." Sheila had to strain her neck to look up at Samson. "I'll have to ask you to leave, and I believe your continued presence here will be a distraction."

"You bet your sweet ass I'll be a distraction. Get out of my way, or I'll have my deputies arrest you."

Sheila looked around for the other agents. All looked away, finding something in the distance of more interest than her predicament. She couldn't count on them for support. They liked Ed, and blamed her for his expulsion. She tried to tell them she had no vote in her destination but it didn't matter. She didn't fight and stepped to one side. The SAC watched Samson, Ed, and Niki cross the small ditch into the area where the body lay.

The medical examiner's office technicians hadn't yet moved the body. They took several dozen photographs and picked up the foreign matter close to the dead girl. It was a useless exercise. Hunters used this area every fall during deer season. Some smoked. Some ate candy or cookies and disposed of the wrappers as they walked. Some randomly fired their shotguns and rifles. Empty shells and cartridges lined the long opening through the woods. They saw pieces of paper and old wrappers everywhere.

Niki stopped and stared at the little girl's headless body. Not only because it was garish, but she wanted to see how the kidnapper had accomplished the feat. The private investigator made a full circle around the crime scene, soaking up every bit of evidence. She determined the kidnapper approached Becky from the back. From the remaining tissue, she discovered the killer held her head with his right hand, and with his left sliced her throat. It took at least two additional attempts before he severed the bone and cartilage. She would know exactly how many after the head was recovered. The investigator noted the missing little finger. The improvised bandage meant it was snipped off while the little girl was still alive. Niki could only shudder at the image, and was more determined than ever.

"What do you have, Little Girl?" Samson used the same pet name for Niki he had since her birth.

"He's a sick puppy. And he's driven by either hatred or revenge. We need to look for enemies of Congressman Howard."

"And you can tell that just by looking at the body?" Ed asked.

"Yes."

She didn't intend to explain her gifts of observation to the ex-SAC.

"They should've put you in my place instead of that worthless piece of flesh," Ed snorted. "You aren't a drunk with no talent."

"If that's the case, why didn't the FBI fire her?" Niki asked.

"Because she's a... she was a high-flying woman. The agency doesn't have enough of them to be politically correct."

"Where do we go now?" Samson asked.

"To recover the rest of Becky."

Niki walked back to the vehicles.

"Hey, what are you doing?"

Yellow police tape surrounded the sedan, part of the crime scene to be analyzed by either the FBI agents or the parish detectives. At one point, Samson and Sheila would have to agree on jurisdiction of the crime scene.

"I'm going to get Becky's head out of the trunk," Niki replied, holding out her hand for the keys.

"What makes you believe it's in the car?" Sheila asked.

"First, it's not a government-issued automobile. My guess is the kidnapper made you switch vehicles."

"But I was with it all the time except for the few minutes it took to find the body. I took the keys with me. No way for him to get in."

"What did he tell you to leave in the trunk? The money?"

"I had one bag left. The other two are at the end of the street in the cul-de-sac. He didn't have time to get any of the bags."

Niki closed her eyes and shook her head.

"Samson, you might want to send a few deputies down there to confirm the other two bags are missing, as well as this one."

"This one isn't missing," Sheila insisted. "I put it in the trunk, and still have the keys."

"Do you really think he would give you a car to drive for which he didn't have a spare set of keys?"

Sheila paled. She hadn't considered a spare set of keys. Still, she couldn't believe it was true. To prove it, she yanked the keys from her pocket and walked to the trunk, sneering at Niki.

"I want an apology from you after I prove just how wrong you are."

Niki showed no sign she heard the woman. Instead, she stared at the trunk of the Impala.

Sheila huffed and inserted the key. With one thrust of the wrist, it popped open. The SAC almost got to the edge of the woods before heaving again.

Niki wasn't surprised to find Becky's head in a box in the trunk of the Impala. It was the only item. The moneybag was nowhere to be found.

"Good call, Little Girl," Samson said. "How did you know?"

"After I discovered the switch in cars, it wasn't hard," Niki replied. "Besides that, there were a couple drops of blood on the bumper. I didn't see any cuts on Sheila."

"That means the murderer was here while Sheila went looking for the child. I'll have to give it to him. He's got a huge set of brass balls," Ed said.

"I don't agree. How much courage does it take to decapitate a small girl?" Niki asked. "He was in no danger while Sheila did her job."

"And in the process of doing that, she left the money and got a child killed."

"The child was doomed from the beginning," Niki replied. "This moron was going to kill her no matter what Sheila did."

"You can call him a moron, but so far, he's outsmarted the best talent of the FBI," Ed said.

"He had better celebrate this victory," Niki said. "I plan on winning the war."

CHAPTER EIGHTEEN

"What's with that gal?" Ed asked Samson after they got back into the squad car.

"What do you mean?"

"She's hell-bent on finding this guy. It's my understanding Congressman Howard fired her."

"Only because he's a dumbass," Samson said. He was free to curse when out of the earshot of Niki.

"What would she have done differently?" Ed asked.

"She wouldn't have given the asshole a dime until she was sure Becky was safe. She wouldn't have fallen for the taped video like Sheila did.

Ed rubbed his hand through his thinning hair.

"I'll agree she's smarter than Sheila. But that doesn't mean much. Most earthworms can make the same claim."

"Why are you holding such a grudge against Sheila? It was the agency that made you retire, not her."

"Because she's the root cause. Just because she's a female, they put me out to pasture."

"What could you have done differently?" Samson asked.

"I would have canvassed the zoo. I would have posted a police broadcast asking anyone there when the child was kidnapped to come forward. I would've figured out a way to trace the phone calls and used a drone to track the money."

"Tracking the money is out. They found the bags," Samson said.

"Where?"

"In the tail car at the parking lot where Sheila last saw it."

"How could he stuff the bags in it with three agents on alert?"

"All three were decapitated."

"The bitch not only let the girl get killed and lost the money, but also lost three agents. On my worst day, that wouldn't have happened."

"I believe you, Ed. This is one of the most fouled-up cases I've seen in a while."

"Or was it fouled up on purpose?" Ed asked.

"What do you mean?"

"Perhaps Sheila set all this up. Someone got real close to those agents without informing them."

Samson nodded, following his logic.

"We only have her word he took all the money. She's the one who supposedly found Becky dead."

"But what about the phone calls? Niki and Congressman Howard said they talked to a man."

After over a minute of silence, he came up with an answer.

"She had an accomplice. Some idiot abetted her."

Samson saw no holes in the ex-SAC's logic. Maybe the retired agent should still be on duty.

CHAPTER NINETEEN

"YOU WANT TO DO WHAT?"

Sheila was back home after the worst day of her life. The urge to take a drink was too strong. The responsibility for telling Congressman Don Howard and his wife about their decapitated daughter had fallen to her. One drink wasn't enough. She was on the third when the doorbell rang. When she saw Samson and six forensic technicians and deputies on her porch, she felt weak, and her knees buckled.

"We're here to serve a search warrant," Samson said. "We got an anonymous tip the ransom money is here."

"You've got to be kidding," the SAC said. "You can't serve that warrant. I'm with the FBI."

"If you don't get out of my way, you'll be in the parish prison. We will search your property."

"You big beast."

Sheila cocked a fist and aimed it at Samson's crotch. The massive chief of homicide wasn't as quick as he had been twenty years earlier. However, he was still quicker than the inebriated agent. Samson caught her fist, swung her around, and cuffed both wrists.

"Put her in the back of a car. We'll let her out after we're finished."

As a deputy led her to the car, other deputies and Samson entered the home. The SAC's place was a mess. The search was into the second hour when a tech called out.

"Samson, you need to see this."

The big chief lumbered to the back porch. On a concrete pad sat three new trash cans. When Samson looked in the first, he knew what the other two held. All three were full of hundred-dollar bills.

CHAPTER TWENTY

"I want to apologize," Sheila said.

She and Niki sat in the interrogation room at the Baton Rouge Sheriff's Office. More than six hours had gone by since the shock of her arrest. Sheila no longer felt the effects of the alcohol. Even in the early morning hours, she remained awake and alert.

"You don't have to do that," Niki said. "Why do you want to see me?"

"I need your help," Sheila said. "I'll admit I was foolish in how I treated you."

"How did the money get into your garbage cans?"

"Somebody put it there. I've been sitting here for hours trying to figure out when they did it."

"Do you have any enemies?"

Sheila snorted.

"Does Baton Rouge have mosquitoes? I've got more than I can count. Most now work for me, or at least they did until a few hours ago."

"Have you been fired?"

"Not yet. I expect to hear from the Bureau any minute now. They can't afford this type of publicity."

"Anyone inside the local office who hates you?"

Another snort.

"Pick a name. They all loved dear ol' Ed. He was a god to them."

"Give me the two most likely suspects," Niki said.

One would be Sid Garrison. Unfortunately, he was the guy behind me in the car I took to Walmart. The kidnapper killed him."

"How about the next two possibles?"

"I'd say Gary Dixon and Dennis Walker. Both have been outspoken in their support of Ed and lack of it for me."

"That gives me a start. One more thing..."

Niki tossed her pencil toward Sheila. The SAC caught it with her right hand and stared as the strawberry blonde left the room.

CHAPTER TWENTY-ONE

Niki arrived at the Baton Rouge FBI office a little after eight the same morning. She knew she could waste no time in her effort to save Sheila Richardson. Not so much from the legal system but more from the other inmates at the parish prison. As soon as they discovered an FBI agent among their ranks, Sheila's life would become worthless.

Gary Dixon was a tall, lean man in his late thirties. To say he was muscular might have been a stretch, but his body held little fat.

"The boss said I had to talk to you," Gary said.

"The boss? Isn't Sheila still in jail?"

"I mean the real boss. Ed is back running the shop on an interim basis. I hope they make it permanent."

"You don't like Sheila?" Niki asked.

"Don't really know her well enough to like or dislike her."

"Then why are you against her?"

"Because she's incompetent. Simple as that. She's not qualified for the job."

"How so?"

"Just like this kidnapping case. She shouldn't have been the one who delivered the money. Protocol says she should have been back here coordinating the operation."

"Do you think Sheila could have set this up?" Niki asked.

Gary paused before answering.

"I'd love to tell you I believed she could, but I can't. She isn't that good."

"What do you mean?"

"Just that. The guy who put this together can predict the behavior of others. Sheila doesn't have that ability."

"Do you?"

Niki watched the agent closely.

Gary shrugged.

"I'll let you know when the Bureau names the next permanent SAC here. That appointment will tell you more than I ever can."

CHAPTER TWENTY-TWO

Dᴇɴɴɪs Wᴀʟᴋᴇʀ ᴅɪᴅɴ'ᴛ ᴍᴇᴇᴛ Niki's expectations of an FBI agent. Short and squat, his ears reminded Niki of Dumbo the Elephant. In his mid-forties, Walker hadn't maintained a rigid diet or exercise regimen. His belly hung a few inches over his belt.

"Tell me about Sheila," Niki said.

"Why?"

"Because she's accused of four murders. Since a kidnapping was involved, she's facing the death penalty."

"Couldn't happen to a nicer person."

"Why do you say that?"

"Because she's a bitch, and you can tell her I said that. I think she knows how I feel, or you wouldn't be here asking me questions."

"Very astute of you, Dennis. Are you always this keen?"

"If you mean, am I smart enough to set up Sheila, then the answer is yes."

"Does that mean you did?"

Dennis shook his head.

"I didn't. Only because it never occurred to me, and I wouldn't kill a girl and three agents."

"Are any other agents capable?"

"Pick one. Every agent in this office is smarter than Sheila Richardson, but of course, that's a pretty low standard."

"I talked with Sheila," Niki said. "I didn't find her to be the complete idiot you describe."

"If Sheila is so smart," the agent said, "then why did she have you fired from the kidnapping case?"

Niki had no answer.

CHAPTER TWENTY-THREE

BEFORE HE LEFT THE BUILDING, Niki dropped in to see the acting SAC of the Baton Rouge office, Ed Samuelson. She knew Ed casually, having attended the same social functions and events in the city.

"This is tough," Niki said.

"Because you're on the wrong side this time."

"Not really. I'm on the side of the truth. If that means Sheila is guilty, then so be it."

"You're working for her. Don't you consider that a conflict of interest with the truth?"

"Not at all," Niki said. "I know for a fact Sheila didn't cut off Becky's head. You can take that to the bank."

"How can you be so certain?"

"I'd rather not say right now."

"What's the matter? Cat got your tongue?"

Both realized the mistake as soon as the words spilled out. He pulled his weapon from its holster, using his left hand. Niki made no move to stop him or protect herself.

"She's right-handed," Niki said. "I see you aren't."

"We don't need to play more games, Niki. You recognized the words I said to you over the phone."

Niki nodded.

"You had to show the Bureau they had made a horrible mistake. You had to show them Sheila couldn't handle the job. You set her up."

"And I had her," Ed responded. "I still do."

"Does that mean you plan to murder me here in your office?"

"One more body won't make a difference. I'll tell everyone you panicked when I told you the FBI wouldn't cut Sheila any slack."

"And they told me you were smart. Sure doesn't look that way to me."

"What do you mean?"

"I've had my phone on since I came in. Samson is listening to every word you're saying."

"I don't believe you," Ed said.

"Talk to him yourself."

Niki extended the phone toward Ed. With his focus on the phone, Niki made a quick chop to Ed's left hand holding the gun. The impact caused his finger to contract, and a shot exploded in the small office. Niki swung a kick into Ed's temple. He tumbled out of his chair and onto the floor.

CHAPTER TWENTY-FOUR

"Do you think it'll work?" Sheila asked.

She and Niki sat in the agent's living room. Niki had made sure no liquor bottles remained in the home.

"I've used this rehab service for clients in the past. It's not quick. You have to do six months at a minimum," Niki replied.

"But I have to go to work."

"My fiancé is a United States senator. He talked with your director. You'll have your old job back if you're sober when you finish the program."

"Why are you helping me after the way I treated you?"

Niki smiled.

"You gave me a second chance to help find little Becky. You deserve one, too."

NOTES

Second Chance is the one of many bullet stories in the Niki Dupre series. It features the dynamic martial arts expert facing even greater challenges.

I have taken a great literary license with the geography and data of Baton Rouge and the surrounding areas. It is a wonderful city and a great way to experience Cajun culture. I live here and find it one of the most desirable places on earth if you enjoy the outdoors, sumptuous cuisine, and remarkable people.

There are so many people to thank:

My family, Linda, Josh, Dalton & Jade

David and Sara Sue

C D and Debbie Smith

My brother and sister-in-law, Bill & Pam

My sister, Debbie

My sister-in-law and her husband, Brenda & Jerry

The Sunday School class at Zoar Baptist

Jeff Trout and Chris Hall, two real men who stood beside me during my darkest hours. Jeff tried to teach me about

Kempo, the ancient Chinese martial art. He soon found out I'm a slow learner.

Any mistakes, typos, and errors are my fault and mine alone. If you would like to get in touch with me, go to my website at http://jimrileyweb.wix.com/jimrileybooks.

Thank you for reading **Second Chance,** and hope you enjoy the rest of my books.

ABOUT THE AUTHOR

Donald Montgomery is a previous winner of The Constable Trophy, awarded by the Scottish Association of Writers. More recently a collection of feel-good stories, set in an affluent retirement complex, Welcome to Somerville Grange, has been published by Next Chapter. Over eighty now, he lives still in the house, near Glasgow, where he was born. He has two daughters, several grandchildren and one wife.

———

To learn more about Jim Riley and discover more Next Chapter authors, visit our website at www.nextchapter.pub.

Second Chance

ISBN: 978-4-82418-258-6

Published by

Next Chapter 合同会社

2-5-6 SANNO

SANNO BRIDGE

143-0023 Ota-Ku, Tokyo

+818035793528

16th June 2023

Milton Keynes UK
Ingram Content Group UK Ltd.
UKHW040108030823
426179UK00003B/53

9 784824 18258